WEBCAM SCAM

BY J. POWELL

illustrated by
Paul Savage

Librarian Reviewer
Joanne Bongaarts
Educational Consultant
MS in Library Media Education, Minnesota State University, Mankato, MN
Teacher and Media Specialist with Edina Public Schools, MN, 1993–2000

Reading Consultant
Elizabeth Stedem
Educator/Consultant, Colorado Springs, CO
MA in Elementary Education, University of Denver, CO

 STONE ARCH BOOKS
Minneapolis San Diego

First published in the United States in 2006
by Stone Arch Books,
151 Good Counsel Drive, P.O. Box 669,
Mankato, Minnesota 56002.
www.stonearchbooks.com

Originally published in Great Britain in 2005
by Badger Publishing Ltd.

Original work copyright © 2005 Badger Publishing Ltd
Text copyright © 2005 Jillian Powell

Library of Congress Cataloging-in-Publication Data
Powell, Jillian.
    Webcam Scam / by J. Powell; illustrated by Paul Savage.
    p. cm.
    "Keystone Books."
    Summary: Carl and his friend Sandy foil the plans of criminals who try
to use a Web reality show scam to cover their burglary.
    ISBN-13: 978-1-59889-011-2 (hardcover)
    ISBN-10: 1-59889-011-5 (hardcover)
    [1. Criminals—Fiction. 2. Fraud—Fiction. 3. Webcams—Fiction.] I.
Savage, Paul, 1971– ill. II. Title.
PZ7.P87755Web 2006
[Fic]—dc22   2005026570

1 2 3 4 5 6 11 10 09 08 07 06

Printed in the United States of America

TABLE OF CONTENTS

Chapter 1

WEB FAMILY

When Carl came home from school,
there was a family meeting going on.

"I think it's really exciting," Mom was saying. "They chose us from a large group of possible families."

"Chose us for what?" Carl asked.

"To be on *The Web Family Show*," Dad smiled at him.

"What's that?" Carl looked blank.

"We're going to appear on the Web," Mom explained. "It's really exciting. We'll be on live webcams, and everyone will get to know us."

"Why us?" Carl didn't like the sound of this at all.

"They said it was because we're just an ordinary family," Mom said.

5

"You and Jo are about the right ages," Mom continued. "They looked at us and liked what they saw."

"No one asked *me*," Carl said. "I don't want everyone spying on me on the Web."

"Come on, Carl," Dad said. "We're all really excited about this. It could be the start of something big."

"Some famous producer might spot me," Jo said.

"What, for a horror movie?" Carl laughed.

"So, do we at least get to see the show?" Carl asked.

"They don't want us watching it," Dad told him. "They want us to just act normal and not think about the cameras and stuff."

Perfect, Carl thought. Every time he popped a pimple or picked his nose, everyone would be watching. Great!

Chapter 2

SET UP

The white van arrived early in the morning. Carl didn't like the look of it. The windows were blackened, and it had a spider web painted on the side. It looked suspicious to Carl.

"They're here!" Mom shouted, sounding excited. "They're putting in the cameras today."

"Can we say where to put them?" Carl asked.

"They know best. They're the experts," Dad told him. "But don't worry, Carl. They won't be showing you in the bathroom. The world's not ready for that."

"Very funny," Carl replied. "Well, I think you're all crazy. It's going to be like living in a fish bowl."

"Who's that strange guy?" Carl added, as a skinny guy wearing shades came up the driveway.

"Watch what you say, Carl," Dad said. "That's the producer. He needs to talk to me and Mom while the crew sets up the cameras. Don't get in the way," he told Carl sharply.

Carl watched as three men wearing white suits jumped out of the van. They carried wire and cameras into the house and began going from room to room. Carl tried to hear what they were saying, but they were talking too quietly. He crept outside the dining room and pressed his ear to the door.

"That would be a good spot. You get a great view. Look!" one man exclaimed.

Carl waited until they moved on.
Then he snuck inside to take a look.
They had put a camera up in the
corner of the room. It was pointing
at the mirror over the fireplace. Carl
stared at the mirror. What was so
interesting about that? Then he looked
into the mirror and saw them — Dad's
silver trophies.

Chapter 3

WEB-EYE

"I'm not supposed to tell you this," Carl told his friend, Sandy. "We had to sign something. It says not to tell anyone. That's weird, don't you think?"

"Are you going to tell me what you're talking about?" Sandy asked. He was trying to get to level six on his new video game, and Carl was making him mess up.

"Okay, here's the deal. We've been chosen to be on *The Web Family Show*," Carl told him. "Our place is stuffed with cameras. And they get to watch us twenty-four seven."

"Why?" Sandy asked. "I mean, not to be funny, but why would anyone want to watch you?"

"Well, exactly. That's my point," Carl said. "I think it's some sort of scam."

"Like what?" Sandy asked.

"I don't know. I just think the men look suspicious. And what exactly are they watching? I mean, there's this camera pointing at a mirror, and when you look in the mirror, what do you see? My dad's silver trophies."

"You think they're casing the joint?" Sandy asked.

"Maybe," said Carl. "We've got to find out."

"Okay, so what's this company called?" asked Sandy.

"Web-Eye, I think," said Carl. "Yeah, that's it!"

"So let's check them out," Sandy told him. "You try getting a phone number, and I'll look them up on the Internet."

An hour later, Carl and Sandy were convinced that Web-Eye didn't exist.

Chapter 4

SABOTAGE

"But Mom —"

"I don't want to hear it, Carl," Mom snapped. "You were against this from the start. Web-Eye may not be listed, but that doesn't mean it doesn't exist. We know it does. We've met the crew."

"We've met some suspicious guy in shades and a team of goons in white suits," Carl said.

"I think it's a scam," added Carl. "They're checking out our house. Sandy says they're casing the joint."

"You told Sandy?" Mom sounded angry. "We aren't supposed to discuss the project. You know that!"

"Why is that?" Carl asked. "We can't watch the show or talk about it. Don't you think that's strange?"

"I don't want to hear any more about it," Mom told him. "And remember, once we get back inside, you're on camera."

How could Carl forget? But if Mom wasn't going to do anything about this, he was. He sent Sandy a text message, asking him to come over.

* * *

"We have to mess with the cameras, pull out the wires or something," Carl said. "But we've got to do it without any of the other cameras seeing us."

"Let's give these snoops something to think about," said Sandy.

When Carl's mom came home, the boys were watching television.

"You boys haven't been messing with the webcams, have you?" Mom asked. "Web-Eye had to send a repair team. The van just arrived."

Carl looked at Sandy. It would take the men a while to find the loose wires. This was their chance to check out the van.

Chapter 5

DISCOVERY

"Hurry up, get inside!" Carl pushed Sandy inside the van and closed the doors behind them.

"It's dark, I can't see," Sandy complained. "Wait a minute. There's a switch here."

Sandy flicked the switch, and a row of television screens lit up.

"Hey, that's our house!" Carl said.

"Look, there's the kitchen, and the dining room, and my bedroom," Carl continued. "Who's that ugly guy?"

"That's the repairman," Sandy said. "He's looking straight into the lens."

"They discovered what we did," Carl said. "We haven't got much time. We've got to find out what's going on here, quick!"

"It's like they're using security cameras," Sandy said. "Like when security guards watch shopping malls. They look at screens like this."

"Yeah, but these aren't security guards, are they?" Carl said. "And if this is going out live on the Web, why are they watching it here in this van? It doesn't make sense."

"Don't know why anyone wants to watch this stuff," Sandy said. "I mean, who wants to stare at your front door?"

"What does it say on there?" Carl peered at the screen showing the front door.

"It's some sort of time log," Sandy said. "Look, it logs all the times you all go out. You, Jo, everyone. They've got some type of software that is reading the times and — "

"That's it!" Carl said suddenly. "Don't you see? They're figuring out the times when the house is going to be empty. And look what you can see on these screens. Dad's silver trophies and Mom's jewelry."

Carl stared at another screen and frowned. "Hey, and all my computer stuff!" he exclaimed.

"It's all listed here, look!" Sandy pointed at another screen. "And there's a floor plan, too. See?"

"Those sneaky . . ."

Carl's words died away. There was a loud bang. The van doors had been slammed shut behind them. The engine started up. The van was leaving with Carl and Sandy inside.

Chapter 6

STOWAWAYS

"Great! What do we do now?"
Sandy whispered.

"Quiet! They'll hear us," Carl said.

"Turn that light off, and move up to
the front. We might hear something,"
Carl added.

The boys moved closer to the front
of the van.

"Something's not right," they heard a gruff voice say. "I never left those wires like that. Looked like someone had been messing with them."

"The sooner we get this job done, the better," another man said.

"We'll do the hit tomorrow," the gruff voice added.

"The dad's at work, the mom goes shopping, the girl goes to her friend's, and that ugly kid goes to karate."

"Judo," Carl whispered. "And who's he calling ugly?"

"Quiet!" Sandy told him.

"You hear anything?" the second man asked.

"Nah. Look. I'm going to pull in here," said the gruff-voiced man. "We're almost out of gas."

"They're stopping," Carl whispered to Sandy. "Wait until the coast is clear. Then jump!"

Chapter 7

A PLAN

"Good thing they needed gas," Sandy said as they headed home. "Otherwise we could have ended up miles away for all we know."

"No, they'll be hanging around here," Carl said. "They're doing the job tomorrow, remember? Well, they're not getting their hands on my computer!"

"You could skip judo," Sandy
suggested. "They're counting on the
house being empty."

"But we can't stay at home forever,
can we?" Carl said. "They'll just keep
trying. We've got to catch them at it."

"Maybe we don't need to catch
them," Sandy said slowly. "Maybe the
webcams will do that for us."

* * *

The next day, when everyone had left, Carl faked his exit. He left by the front door, then ducked around the block, and climbed back over the fence into his backyard.

He looked at his cell phone. There was a text message from Sandy.

VAN HERE. LOOK OUT.

Carl climbed back in through the window he had left open and hid under the stairs. After a few minutes, he heard a noise. Then voices.

"You sure you killed the master switch?" one of them asked. "Okay, make it quick then. Start with the silver trophies."

Carl's fingers fumbled with his phone in the dark. Sandy should be inside the van by now.

```
THEY'RE IN. GET CAMERAS
BACK ON. LOOK FOR MASTER
SWITCH.
```

Seconds later, there was a reply.

```
MASTER ON. POLICE ON WAY.
```

"Don't forget the kid's computer," he heard a voice say. "There's some decent stuff there."

Smile, Carl thought. *You're on camera.*

Chapter 8

"YOU'RE UNDER ARREST"

Carl waited for what seemed like hours. Then he heard voices, but it was only the men coming downstairs.

"Good job," he heard one say. "Like stealing candy from a baby. This Web game is really going to work."

"Quiet!" another man said. "Did you hear something outside? I think someone's coming back. Hide under the stairs, quick!"

Carl held his breath. He was about to have company.

"Stop right there!" a new and loud voice said. "You're under arrest!"

"We- we're here to work on the cameras," one of the men sputtered.

"Oh, we know all about the cameras," the police officer said. "Nice of you to record your crime for us. Makes our job much easier."

"Well done, Sandy," smiled the police officer. "You cracked a tricky scam here."

Sandy wasn't getting all of the credit. Carl came out from under the stairs.

"Here's another one," the police officer said, grabbing Carl by the arm. "He's the one who broke in through that window. It's all on camera."

"No, that's Carl. He lives here," Sandy explained.

"Oh, right. Well, neat job, boys," the police officer said. "A lot neater than that bedroom of yours, Carl," he added with a grin.

"From now on, no one gets to see my room except me," Carl said. Anyway, who had time to clean bedrooms when he and Sandy were busy busting webcam scams?

ABOUT THE AUTHOR

Jillian Powell started writing when she was very young. She loved having a giant pad of paper and some pens or crayons in front of her. She made up newspaper stories about jewel thieves and spies. Jillian's parents still have her early stories, complete with crayon illustrations!

ABOUT THE ILLUSTRATOR

Paul Savage works in a design studio, drawing pictures for advertising. He says illustrating books is "the best job." He's always been interested in illustrating books, and he loves reading. Paul also enjoys playing sports and running.

He lives in England with his wife and daughter, Amelia.

GLOSSARY

Internet (IN-tur-net)—a network that allows millions of computers around the world to connect together

producer (pruh-DOO-sur)—a person in charge of making a movie or TV program

sabotage (SAB-uh-tahzh)—to damage something on purpose

scam (SKAM)—a plan to steal from or trick someone

software (SAWFT-wair)—programs that control a computer

stowaway (STOH-uh-way)—someone who hides in a vehicle without others knowing

webcam (WEB-kam)—a camera that shows pictures on the Internet or Web

DISCUSSION QUESTIONS

1. Right away, Carl has doubts about *The Web Family Show*. What things make Carl suspicious about the Web-Eye crew?

2. Carl tries to tell his family that the Web-Eye crew is up to no good. Why do you think Carl's family ignores his warnings?

3. Do you think the Web-Eye crew robbed other people? If so, why weren't they caught until they tried to scam Carl's family?

WRITING PROMPTS

1. Imagine that your family has just been chosen to be on *The Web Family Show*. Would you want to be on the show? Write why or why not.

2. The Web-Eye crew wanted the family's most valuable possessions. Make a list of your belongings that mean the most to you. Write why you would not want to lose them.

ALSO BY
J. POWELL

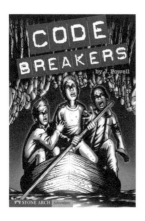

Code Breakers
1-59889-010-7

One ordinary afternoon, three friends find a strange briefcase on a park bench. Discover the danger and adventure that await them as the boys decide to follow the mysterious clues they find inside the case.

5010 Calling
1-59889-012-3

Beta lives in the year 5010, and many things are different about his world. What happens when he taps into the mind of Zac, who lives in 2000? What does he learn about the past? And what does Zac learn about the future?

OTHER BOOKS
IN THIS SET

Steel Eyes
by Jonny Zucker
1-59889-019-0

Emma Stone is the new girl in school. Why does she always wear sunglasses? Gail and Tanya are determined to find out, but Emma's cold stare is more than they bargained for.

Splitzaroni
by K. I. White
1-59889-014-X

Naseem always runs for cover when his mom returns with the groceries. When she comes back with a weird new plant, it seems she might have gone too far.

INTERNET SITES

Do you want to know more about subjects related to this book? Or are you interested in learning about other topics? Then check out FactHound, a fun, easy way to find Internet sites.

Our investigative staff has already sniffed out great sites for you!

Here's how to use FactHound:

1. Visit *www.facthound.com*

2. Select your grade level.

3. To learn more about subjects related to this book, type in the book's ISBN number: **1598890115**.

4. Click the **Fetch It** button.

FactHound will fetch the best Internet sites for you!